Goosey Bump: Nappy Doll

Horror Collection

Tenisha Bullock

COPYRIGHTS

Paperback - ISBN: 978-1-970686-00-5
Hardcover - ISBN: 978-1-970686-01-2

DEDICATION

To Lorenzo Gardner Sr., for never letting go of my hand.

ACKNOWLEDGEMENT

First, I thank God, the author of every open door and every victory. I am grateful for my support system, who kept me lifted when the path was steep, and for my sister, whose love and honesty steady my steps. To every reader who wrestles with doubt, take heart and keep going. All things are possible with God.

ABOUT THE AUTHOR

Tenisha Bullock is a dynamic Urban Culture Artist and devoted woman of God whose work blends creativity, faith, and community service. Her art and story have been featured in publications including Canvas Rebel, Bold Journey, Artist Closeup, and Authority Magazine, and her pieces have appeared in shows, art walks, auctions, and the Red River Revel.

Beyond the studio, Tenisha mentors youth and seniors, creates a local newspaper comic in Bogalusa, Louisiana, and organizes community events that champion hope and resilience.

An entrepreneur and small transportation business owner, Tenisha is also pursuing a Bachelor of Science in Psychology with a focus in clinical and marriage therapy within evangelical ministries, with graduation expected in April 2026.

She believes in combining lived experience, academic insight, and ministry to cultivate transformative leadership, especially among women and girls.

Tenisha is the author of It's Not How You Start This Race, an inspirational book, and Lily and the Magic Seed, a children's picture book available on Amazon. Her mission is simple and bold: help people discover their God-given gifts, heal what hurts, and step into purpose.

She leads by example, turning hardship into fuel, and stands as proof that a life of faith and art can change communities one story at a time.

Contents

The Gift That Shouldn't Have Arrived 11
Smile Wide, Nappy 16
Charm Bracelet of Secrets 20
Miss Mumu: The Rag Doll Who Weeps 24
Interlude 31
"The Doll That Sang to the Dead" 35
She Cries for You 42
The Last Tear 48
Velvet Vee: The Doll That Dances with Shadows – Part I 54
HYMN: The Doll That Sings in Shadows 61
WHISPER: The Doll That Speaks Secrets 66
Velvet Vee: The Doll That Dances with Shadows – Part II 72
Mr. Greeley's Last Stand 80
The Secret of Madame Borscht 86
Echoes in the Dark 96
The Hunt Begins 100
Hymn's Lullaby 104
Shadow Pox's Cold Grip 107

The Mother Doll's Return 111

Home At Last 116

The Quiet Dollhouse..119

Miss Maw Awakens..125

PROLOGUE

There is a locked room beneath Maple Street Elementary. It smells like warm dust and old metal. On a shelf sit narrow boxes lined with salt and iron. Mr. Greeley keeps the key on a chain and checks the seals one by one, listening for sounds a box should never make.

His notebook is small and careful.

Mumu. Weeps. Do not let her fill the pail.
Hymn. Do not wind.
Whisper. Feed her nothing.
Velvet Vee. Never dance alone.
Shadow Pox. Treat the air like a surface.
Mother. Break the light at her chest.

He closes the book. The school above him is quiet, but quiet is not safe. He learned that the night a lullaby walked up his old stairs.

There are rules for dolls like these. Do not take them home. Do not hide what they tell you. Do not look for them in mirrors. If water gathers where there are no pipes, leave. If a locked music box begins to play, do not listen. If a doll blinks, believe it.

Across town, a cardboard parcel waits on a child's shelf, ribbon tied neat. In an attic, a wooden trunk shifts a little in its sleep. In a props closet, a velvet hat tips in the dark. In a swamp, frost climbs a reed and pulls back like a held breath.

Mr. Greeley locks the door and says it will hold through the night. He does not believe it. Curses do not end. They change shape.

The ribbon loosens on the waiting box. A nightlight shrinks to a thin coin on the carpet. A whisper lifts like breath on glass.

I like your tears.

Rain thickens. The town settles. Painted eyes stay open.

If you are careful, you pass a shelf of dolls and feel nothing at all. If you are unlucky, one follows you home without moving an inch.

Remember the simple things. Locks keep doors shut. Salt keeps circles whole. Stories keep children awake long enough to live. And when the night is not kind, you will hear the rhyme first.

Prologue Rhyme

"In Grandma's attic, lined with lace,
A hundred dolls stare into space.
They whisper secrets, dark and deep,
And guard your dreams when you're asleep.
But break the rules or tell a lie—
And one will blink before you die."

CHAPTER 1

The Gift That Shouldn't Have Arrived

"A gift wrapped tight in black and red,
From loving hands now cold and dead.
Open slow, and don't you cry—
A doll once hugged may say goodbye."

. . .

It all started with the accident.

One minute, Grandma Addie was humming in her car, headed to buy a special gift for her five-year-old granddaughter, Nia.

The next minute

A deer.

Screeching tires.

Broken glass.

Silence.

The car flipped twice.

By the time the ambulance arrived, Grandma Addie was gone.

But the package in the seat beside her? Still there. Not even a scratch on the box.

Two weeks later, it arrived on Nia's doorstep. No note. No return address. Just her name, written in Grandma's perfect handwriting

To my sweet Nia. For your birthday. Always remember—you are special.

XOXO—Love, Grandma A.

Nia's parents, still grieving, placed the unopened box on her bookshelf.

It sat there for days.

Watching.

Waiting.

It was late Sunday night, the wind howling outside like a pack of wolves. Nia sat cross-legged in her bed, staring at the box. She felt a strange pull, like the box was calling her.

Maybe Grandma wanted her to open it.

Maybe it would make the sadness go away.

She pulled it into her lap, untied the black ribbon, and peeled away layers of soft, pink tissue paper.

Inside was a doll.

But not like the ones at toy stores.

She had warm brown skin, long curls, big blinking brown eyes with lashes, and a purple lace dress. Her smile was tiny, like it was shy. Around her wrist, a single heart charm bracelet.

"She's pretty," Nia whispered.

The doll blinked.

Just once.

Nia dropped her.

It landed softly on the carpet, facedown.

She stared at it; breath caught in her throat.

"I didn't see that," she whispered to herself. "It didn't blink."

She picked it up again.

The doll's smile looked slightly... wider.

But maybe she was imagining things.

She pulled the covers up and laid the doll next to her.

“I think I’ll name you Nappy.”

The room was quiet.

Nappy didn’t say a word.

But as Nia closed her eyes, she heard something faint.

“I like that name.”

LOVE

CHAPTER TWO

Smile Wide, Nappy

"If you hear her bracelet ring,
She's awake and watching things.
If you draw her, draw her true—
Or she just might redraw you."

. . .

The next morning, Nia woke to the sound of something dragging on the floor.

Scccrrraaatch.

Her room was too dark. Way too dark. She blinked at the clock: 9:23 a.m. It should've been bright by now.

She sat up and screamed.

Her walls were covered in black crayon drawings.

Sloppy spirals. Angry stick figures. Crossed-out eyes. In the center, drawn above her bed, was a little girl holding hands with a doll.

The girl had Xs for eyes.

And the doll?

Smiling wider than ever.

Nia turned her head slowly toward the nightstand.

Nappy was gone.

"Nappy?" she whispered.

No answer.

She scanned the floor. Nothing.

Then she heard it.

Creeeeeeaaaaak.

The closet.

The door eased open, inch by inch, until it stopped.

And there, sitting at the back of the closet...

Nappy.

A black crayon sat in her lap.

Her bracelet gleamed.

Later that morning, Nia's mother was horrified by the mess.

"Nia Simone, what on earth?!"

"I didn't do it! It was Nappy!"

“Nia… no more spooky stories. I’m throwing this creepy thing away.”

She snatched Nappy off the floor and stormed out.

Nia tried to shout, “Don’t touch her!”

But the words stuck in her throat.

She saw the doll’s face change, just for a second.

That sweet, tiny smile?

Now it was a snarl.

A warning.

That night, rain fell hard and fast. The trash can sat at the curb, lid shut tight.

But Nia couldn’t sleep.

She kept watching the window.

At 2:37 a.m., the lid slid open.

A shadow climbed out and dropped to the sidewalk.

Tiny.

Doll-sized.

A bracelet shimmered in the rain.

The next morning, Nia's mother looked... strange.

Her eyes were bloodshot. Her skin pale.

"Morning, baby," she said in a tired voice. "Mommy's just... not feeling like herself."

Nia didn't answer.

She was staring at the counter.

Where Nappy sat.

Dry. Clean.

Smiling.

And now there was another charm on her bracelet.

A tiny gold charm.

It looked like...

a screaming face.

CHAPTER THREE

Charm Bracelet of Secrets

"Count the charms and hear them chime,

One for sorrow, two for crime.

Three for pain, and four for dread—

Five means someone ends up dead."

. . .

The day after Nappy returned, the house got colder.

Even though the thermostat said seventy-four degrees, Nia's room felt like the inside of a freezer. Her breath fogged the mirror. Her toys stopped working. Lights flickered when she walked by.

Her mom didn't notice. She barely even blinked anymore.

Nia knew why.

It was Nappy.

Each night, Nia heard whispers.

Not from the doll's mouth... but from the charm bracelet.

It jingled in the dark, and each time, a new charm appeared.

A broken heart.

A small pair of scissors.

A doll-sized teardrop.

A cracked clock face.

And now, a fifth charm had appeared, one shaped like an eye, wide and watching.

That's when Nia decided.

She had to destroy the doll.

That night.

She waited until her mom was asleep, then crept into the kitchen and pulled the matches from the junk drawer.

Nappy sat on the counter, smiling. Silently.

"I'm sorry, Grandma," Nia whispered. "But this isn't a gift. It's a curse."

She carried the doll into the backyard and placed her in the rusty old grill.

The clouds above twisted like they were watching.

Nia struck the match.

Held it to the paper towel she'd tucked under Nappy's lace dress.

The fire caught. And Nappy started to burn.

At first... nothing happened.

Then—

SSSSHHHHHHRIEK!!!

The flames screamed.

A high, sharp, twisting sound like a hundred voices trapped in a glass jar.

Nia stumbled back as black smoke poured into the sky.

Nappy's eyes melted.

The bracelet snapped.

And the last thing Nia saw before she passed out...

was a cloud of dark smoke floating up...

...then splitting off...

...floating over the backyard fence...

...toward the school playground.

The next morning

Nia woke in her bed.

The grill was empty.

No doll. No ashes. No bracelet.

Her mom was downstairs making waffles—smiling like nothing had happened.

"Did you sleep okay, sweet girl?"

Nia nodded slowly. "Yeah... better."

The house felt warmer, brighter. Almost normal again.

But miles away, across town...

at an elementary school playground...

something was lying half-burnt in the sandbox.

A soft cloth rag doll.

Missing one button eye.

Covered in dirt.

And as a child walked by and picked her up, a faint whisper rose on the wind: "I like your tears."

CHAPTER FOUR

Miss Mumu: The Rag Doll Who Weeps

"In the sand she hides her face,
A soggy dress, torn bits of lace.
She cries for you when skies turn black—
And if you leave... she'll want you back."

. . .

Kori Washington never liked recess.

It wasn't the heat, or the noise, or even the sticky monkey bars.

It was the kids.

She just didn't fit in.

They called her "Crybaby Kori," because she teared up when the teachers shouted. Because her eyes always watered when it rained. Because she once cried in the lunch line when her spaghetti fell off the tray.

So today, she stayed far away from the games and laughter. She wandered toward the edge of the playground, by the big sycamore tree and the sandbox no one used anymore.

That's when she saw it.

Half-buried in the sand...

A doll.

Soft. Cloth. Rag-style. Like something from a long time ago. Her dress was soaked and stained, her face dirty. One eye was a shiny black button. The other? Torn off, just loose threads.

Kori picked her up and brushed off the dirt.

The doll was cold.

But... warm at the same time. Like holding something that had a heart inside it.

"What the..." Kori whispered.

Another tear dropped.

It hit the sand with a hiss, like steam.

Kori stuffed the doll in her backpack and brought her home.

She didn't know why. It just felt like the right thing to do.

No one greeted her when she got there, her mom was on another video call, her dad wasn't home, and her older sister barely looked up from her phone.

Kori pulled out the doll and sat her on the bed.

She noticed a name stitched into the back of the doll's dress.

Faded, but still readable

"MISS MUMU,"

Kori shivered.

The rain picked up outside, tapping the window like a soft knock.

She looked back at the doll.

Now there were three teardrops rolling down Miss Mumu's cloth cheek.

"Why are you crying?" Kori asked.

Miss Mumu didn't answer.

But the rain?

It got louder.

The Flood

That night, Kori dreamt of water.

She was walking through her school hallway, except it was underwater. Books floated past her head. Desks flipped upside down. She saw fish swimming in the library.

And at the far end of the hall, knee-deep in shadowy floodwater...

Miss Mumu stood perfectly still.

Her torn button eye gleamed like a marble.

When Kori tried to run, the water rose up.

She woke up screaming.

Her bed was soaked.

Not just damp, soaked. Her blankets, her pillows, her carpet.

There was a puddle under the doll.

Miss Mumu was still crying.

The First Revenge

At school the next day, Kori sat alone during lunch, Miss Mumu tucked safely in her backpack.

That's when Raelyn and Jaz, the mean girls from class, marched over.

“Is it true you brought a wet doll to school?” Raelyn sneered.

“You gonna cry again, Crybaby?” Jaz laughed.

They snatched Kori’s backpack and unzipped it.

Miss Mumu stared up at them.

“Ew!” Raelyn gagged. “She smells like moldy soup!”

They threw the doll into the mud.

“Oops. Guess she’s still crying.”

The girls laughed and walked away.

Kori ran to the doll, heart pounding.

But Miss Mumu wasn’t muddy.

She was dry.

And warm.

And smiling.

Her button eye was glowing now.

That night, the storm came.

Loud. Violent. Endless.

Rain hammered the roof. Lightning cracked across the sky. Wind howled like screaming voices.

Kori woke up to her phone buzzing. It was a text from the school.

"Due to flooding in the east wing, classes are CANCELED."

She blinked in the dark.

Something was... moving outside her window.

A rush of water poured past, like a river.

She opened the curtain.

And screamed.

Her school, just across the street, was flooded.

Water poured through the front doors.

And in that rising floodwater...

She saw Raelyn's pink sparkly backpack floating.

Then Jaz's jacket.

And standing at the front gate, completely dry, was Miss Mumu.

SMILING.

WELCOME

Interlude

"In the sand she hides her face,
A soggy dress, torn bits of lace.
She cries for you when skies turn black—
And if you leave... she'll want you back."

The next day, even though the school was flooded, parents still dropped kids off; teachers herded them into the dry half of the building for indoor recess.

Kori sat on the edge of the hallway, clutching her backpack tightly. Miss Mumu was inside. And for the first time... Kori was afraid to let her out.

The other kids whispered:

"Did you hear about the east wing?"

"The lockers exploded."

"Someone said they saw footprints in the water."

"Like... doll-sized."

Kori's stomach twisted.

Just then, the hallway lights buzzed.

Flicker. Flicker. Snap.

One went out.

Then another.

And from the dark end of the hallway came the squeak... squeak... squeak... of a janitor's cart.

A shadow rounded the corner, pushing the old metal cart like it weighed a thousand pounds.

It was Mr. Greeley.

Most kids avoided him. He barely spoke. Wore the same gray jumpsuit every day, black gloves on his hands, and a janitor's key ring so big it looked like it could unlock dungeons.

But today... he stopped.

Right in front of Kori.

His eyes were small and sunken, like two brown marbles under his wrinkled forehead. He looked at her. Then at her backpack.

"You feel it yet?" he said in a voice like gravel and cough syrup.

Kori froze. "F-feel what?"

He leaned in, whispering.

"The crying in your bones. The air growing thick. That doll in your bag isn't just old, girl. It remembers."

Kori opened her mouth to ask how he knew, but Mr. Greeley cut her off.

He reached into his cart and pulled something out.

A tiny, scorched wooden hand. Doll-sized. Charred black.

"She had a sister once," he said. "Back in 1989. Came with eyes made of glass and a mouth that sang lullabies when you were alone."

He held the blackened hand up to the light.

"I tried to burn her. Thought I did."

He lowered it slowly.

"But dolls like these, they don't burn. They just... move on."

Kori's throat was dry. "What do they want?"

Mr. Greeley's face darkened. His voice dropped to a whisper so quiet it felt like the walls were listening.

"To be loved. To be held. To be cried for."

He stared at her backpack again. "Yours is still collecting tears. When it fills up..." He shuddered. "She'll decide."

Kori whispered, "Decide what?"

But Mr. Greeley was already walking away.

As his cart squeaked down the hall, he called back without turning:

"Keep her close if you want to live. But don't let her cry too long. Or she'll MAKE SOMEONE CRY FOR HER."

CHAPTER FIVE

"The Doll That Sang to the Dead"

"If your doll begins to hum,
Run away; don't tell your mom.
When lullabies come soft and slow,
She's calling to the ones below."

. . .

Back then, his name wasn't "Mr. Greeley."

It was just John. John Greeley, widowed, thirty-nine, tired but still holding on to joy. He had one joy left in the world.

His daughter, Lila.

She was seven. Bright. Loved puzzles and painting. She drew smiley faces on everything, even the old mailbox out front.

John worked in a toy shop, one of those magical old places with real wood floors and a little bell on the door. He made toys by hand: puppets, jack-in-the-boxes, wooden animals.

And one day, after six months of carving and stitching, he made something new.

A doll.

A cloth doll with glass eyes, a silk dress, and a tiny music box stitched into her chest.

"I made her for you, Lila," he said on her birthday. "She sings just for you."

The doll's name, stitched into her tag in silver thread:

"HYMN"

At first, Lila loved her.

She carried Hymn everywhere, tied a bow in her yarn hair, and kissed her goodnight.

When she pulled the string on the doll's back, it played a lullaby no one recognized.

"Hush now, hush, no need to fear…

The dark can't reach you when I'm near…"

Soft. Slow. Soothing.

But by the third week, the song... changed.

It got slower.

Lower.

And the last note never quite ended, it just hung there like a foghorn in the dark.

Lila started waking up screaming. "She sings while I'm sleeping!"

John would rush in, but the doll would be still. Quiet.

"Nightmares," he told himself.

But then the paintings started.

Lila's crayons filled page after page, black shadows, figures in windows, faces without eyes.

One morning, she handed him a drawing.

"It's Mommy," she said softly. "Hymn says she wants to come home."

John dropped the picture.

Because the figure beside Lila in the drawing, tall, pale, and wearing a tattered veil, looked exactly like his dead wife.

The Night of the Fire

The final night came during a thunderstorm.

Lila wouldn't eat. Wouldn't talk. She just sat in the corner with Hymn in her lap, humming the tune over and over again.

And when John leaned in to take the doll away, she bit him.

Not Lila. The doll.

Its glass eyes flicked toward him. Its mouth stretched wider.

John screamed and threw it across the room. Thunder cracked. The power went out.

In the dark, Lila whispered,

"She says you took her from the wrong place."

Then all the windows shattered at once.

He grabbed a hammer, lit a match, and ran for the fireplace.

The doll tried to crawl.

He shoved it into the flames.

The lullaby screamed.

The fire hissed black smoke and burst.

Lila collapsed. Unmoving.

The doll's glass eyes exploded in the fire.

When John pulled his daughter away, her hands were cold.

Just a faint hum from her lips, repeating the last line:

"The dark can't reach you when I'm near..."

After the incident, John Greeley was never the same.

His hands burned from the fire, scars he still covers with gloves.

He quit the toy shop. Took a job in a school where no dolls were allowed.

Or so he thought.

Until he saw one again.

Years later.

In the sandbox.

Crying.

And he knew... the lullabies had never really stopped.

Back to the Present

The bell rang somewhere in the distance.

Mr. Greeley blinked hard and realized he'd stopped pushing his cart. He was just standing there in the empty east wing of the school.

Alone.

The lights buzzed above. Rain tapped gently against the cracked windowpane.

He looked down at the small, blackened hand he still kept in his tool belt.

The one from Hymn.

He thought of Lila, her tiny laugh, her drawings, her warm little fingers now gone cold.

And then he thought of the girl from earlier, Kori.

He'd seen it before.

That look in her eyes.

"Too late," he whispered. "It's happening again."

Water began to pool at the edges of the floor.

He didn't even hear the faucet running.

CHAPTER SIX

She Cries for You

"Her sorrow flows from seam to seam,
Soaked in rage and stitched with screams.
If you don't dry her eyes each night,
She'll flood your world with endless fright."

. . .

Kori didn't tell anyone about the flood at school.

Not the backpack. Not the whispering rain. Not the glowing button eye.

She just... stopped talking.

Her words felt waterlogged, too heavy to lift.

And the crying? It got worse.

Sleep thinned to a film. Every blink was a shore she could not reach.

Each night, her bedroom floor slicked over with cold water that didn't come from pipes.

Shoes: soaked. Notebooks: warped to waves. Posters bubbled off the paint like blisters.

The wall beside her bed grew damp. The sockets hissed. Paint blistered, peeled, and fell, white scales in the dark.

Miss Mumu sat beside her, bone dry. The single button eye caught the moon and refused to let it go.

By morning, a fresh puddle glowed under the doll, as if the floor were trying to breathe.

Miss Mumu's List

By Friday, three students had gone home "sick."

Raelyn: fever. Chills. A cough that sounded full of water.

Jaz: woke up screaming, swore something was tugging her down through the mattress springs.

Elijah: slipped in a hallway puddle and broke his wrist, except there was no leak, no warning cone, just footprints. Doll-sized. Then gone.

Kori's stomach turned to ice.

She looked at the doll. Then at her notebook.

She printed a title in block letters, the letters looked like they were drowning as the ink spread.

WHO MADE ME CRY

- *RAELYN*
- *JAZ*
- *MR. TANAKA (gym teacher)*
- *MAKENZIE (sister)*
- *Me (A LOT)*

Miss Mumu blinked.

A tear stitched itself down her cheek and fell onto the page.

The ink ran like veins in water.

Warning Signs

Mr. Greeley found her after school in the library stacks no one used.

Miss Mumu sat in Kori's lap. The doll was warm the way a fever is warm.

Mr. Greeley slid onto the carpet across from her and pulled a palm-sized notebook from his pocket.

The cover was cracked, the paper warping from old damp. A label on the front:

"DOLL LOG: Entry 47 — MUMU."

He inched it over. "You're not the first."

Kori stroked the doll's cloth hand. "She hasn't... hurt me."

"Yet," he said softly. The word landed like a drop into a deep well.

"What does she want?"

He glanced at the ceiling as if listening for storm drain pipes. "Someone to carry her grief. That one's stitched from sorrow. She feeds on pain."

"But she protects me," Kori said, barely audible.

"No, child." His eyes were tired. "She's training you."

Silence. Then.

Drip. Drip. Drip.

Black water bulged from the ceiling grid and gathered above them, a dark bubble trembling with weight.

Kori screamed as the drop fell. It hit the log and spidered across the ink.

Miss Mumu tilted her head, smiling with thread.

The Bathroom Incident

Makenzie picked Kori up late. "You didn't pack your gym clothes again?" she groaned. "God, you're such a little freak lately."

Kori's jaw locked. "I'll walk home."

Makenzie rolled her eyes and shouldered into the girls' bathroom.

Ten minutes. Then the janitor's radio crackled:

"Uh... we've got a situation. West wing. Girls' bathroom."

The door was flooded shut. Water curled out from under it like steam in reverse.

When they finally forced it, a warm wave sloshed over the threshold and slapped their shoes.

Makenzie crouched on the sink, soaked, hair pasted to her cheeks, eyes huge and red. She kept whispering one word.

"Doll."

Final Warning

Mr. Greeley cornered Kori the next morning by the supply closet, raincoat dripping though the sky was clear.

"You have to let her go."

"I can't," Kori snapped. "She's not hurting me."

"You're wrong," he said, and peeled off a glove.

Kori's breath hitched.

His palm was a ruin, shiny, ridged, a melted map. Scar tissue webbed the knuckles like wax gone wrong.

"This," he said, "is what happens when you try to burn pain. Some grief doesn't leave. It settles."

He held her gaze.

"And it will wear you like a doll if you let it."

CHAPTER SEVEN

The Last Tear

"Her arms are soft, her heart is stone,

She'll cry for you when you're alone.

But dry her eyes before the night,

Or she will take your soul in spite."

. . .

Kori fell asleep with the doll in her arms. She hadn't meant to. Exhaustion pulled her under; the whispers did the rest.

The dream was her room.

Only wrong.

Water climbed the wallpaper like ivy with fingers. Fast. The nightlight fizzed and spit. The floorboards lifted like boat planks, creaking as if something swam beneath.

Miss Mumu sat on the dresser, legs neatly folded. She hummed a lullaby that sounded like a throat full of water.

"Why are you doing this?" Kori cried, and her voice came back to her from the drain.

"Because you're the saddest of them all," Mumu whispered. "And you still don't want to cry."

The overhead bulb went black. The room sank.

Kori gasped—woke—

DRENCHED.

Sheets floated, pale jellyfish. Her pillow bobbed. Her hair clung to her neck like weed.

On the nightstand, the doll waited. Dry. Listening.

Mr. Greeley's Final Choice

Kori ran through rain that needle-stitched her skin.

The school loomed. Midnight leaked from the gutters.

She pounded on the janitor's door under the bleachers.

It opened immediately. He hadn't been sleeping. He didn't sleep.

"She's going to drown me," Kori sobbed. "She says I'm the saddest. I'm the one she wants."

He sighed, a sound like a tide going out, and crossed to a high shelf.

He pulled down a box wrapped in twine that had absorbed other storms. Inside,

- • An old charm bracelet.
- A cracked porcelain eye.
- A scorched music box.
- And a cloth square, blue and faded, labeled

DRY CLOTH — ONLY USE ONCE

He handed her the cloth.

"You have to wipe away her last tear," he said. "The one she stitched from your sadness."

"If I do?"

"She'll either disappear," he said, quieter, "or... wear you like a doll's skin."

The Final Cry

Kori waded into her house. The water in the hallway reached her shins and tugged at her shoelaces like small hands.

In her room, Miss Mumu sat on the pillow. Water pooled beneath her in a cold halo.

"I'm ready," Kori said, voice shaking but steady.

The stitched mouth pinched. "Are you sure you want to forget what hurts?"

Kori pulled the blue cloth from her pocket. It felt warm, as if it remembered other tears.

"You don't understand," Kori screamed. "I'm not sad because I'm weak. I'm sad because I care. I cry because I feel. That doesn't belong to you."

She reached out...

A single tear rolled down Miss Mumu's cheek.

Kori wiped it gently with the cloth.

For a heartbeat, the whole house held its breath.

The tear brightened, mercury light, then vanished into the weave.

The air uncoiled. No more dripping. No more hum.

The room dried between one blink and the next.

The pillow dented and rose.

The doll was— Gone.

Aftermath

Kori didn't sleep that night.

She watched the corners for movement all anxious.

But morning came dry.

Sun pooled on the floor. Her backpack was light.

It was over.

Outside, the storm had finally given the sky back.

Across town, in the school sandbox, something blinked under a crust of damp sand.

A new doll waited, porcelain face, velvet hat, painted red lips, buried to the chin.

Eyes wide open.

CHAPTER EIGHT

Velvet Vee: The Doll That Dances with Shadows – Part 1

"When velvet feet begin to glide,
Watch the shadows swell and slide.
Dance alone or dance with me—
But don't get lost... she's never free."

. . .

The Props Closet

The old community theater was full of forgotten things.

Broken seats scabbed with gum.

Dust-choked curtains that coughed when you pulled them.

Spiderwebs stitched like funeral lace across the rafters.

But the strangest secret lived behind a warped door labeled PROPS.

At least, that's what Emily told herself as she slipped inside after rehearsal, no lights, just a cobalt ribbon of dusk through the high window.

The air tasted like old perfume and mouse droppings. Paper programs curled on the floor, their dates yellowed to the color of teeth.

Emily loved to dance. Her dream was to star in the spring musical. Lately, though, her turns landed like half-memories. Something was missing. A partner she couldn't see.

She rummaged through hatboxes and costume racks that sighed like sleeping things. Her fingers brushed velvet; cold, soft, wrong, and came up with a tiny hat rimmed in black beads. Beneath it lay a doll.

Porcelain face. Painted lips, just a little too red. A black velvet dress that caught the dim light and refused to give it back.

On her chest, stitched in silver thread, a dancing shoe.

A tag. Velvet Vee.

Emily didn't mean to smile. She just did.

The doll did, too.

First Dance

Emily hugged Velvet Vee close. The velvet felt damp, like breath through fabric.

At home, she set the doll on the dresser and cued her practice playlist.

She leapt. Turned. Landed.

Something moved with her.

At first, it was just the ordinary shadow her lamp made. But then the shadow stretched, thinned, and slipped a beat behind her.

Another joined it, then another, each a little slower, a little hungrier. They tried her steps, copied her arms, lagged like tired partners tugging at her wrists.

Emily spun to a stop, dizzy.

The room kept moving.

Velvet Vee's button eyes caught the light like slick oil.

In the glass, Emily saw herself, alone, except she didn't feel alone at all.

She felt... chosen. Scared & numb.

The Shadow's Grip

By Friday, the circles under Emily's eyes had gone the color of plum bruises.

"Why are you always so tired?" her friends asked.

"You keep bumping into, like, everything."

"Who are you talking to in the wings?"

That night, the whisper came from the corner where the dresser stood.

Dance… dance with me…

Velvet Vee sat perfectly still. The shadows around her didn't. They unspooled up the wall in long black ribbons, braiding into fingers. Then hands. Then claws that pinched the light and made it bleed.

Emily shoved the doll into a drawer and slammed it shut.

For a breath, silence.

Then the velvet hat, wedged under the dresser, tilted. The moon snagged on its beadwork.

Emily's knees unlocked. Her feet slid to first position without permission.

Her legs began to move. She had no choice.

The Final Performance

The auditorium packed itself to the rafters, parents, teachers, rows of little phones like staring eyes.

Backstage, Emily's heart hammered high in her throat. Velvet Vee waited in the shadow of the grand drape, not where Emily had left her. The doll's head had turned, just enough to watch.

The music started.

Emily stepped into the wash of stage light. Heat wrapped her shoulders. The floor felt slicker than marley, like something under it was breathing.

The first phrases were clean. The audience hushed. A good hush.

Then the wings darkened, as if the curtains had grown taller. Shadows slid out, barely there, like smoke with fingers.

They coiled around Emily's ankles and tugged, gentle at first, then insistent, like partners steering a dance she hadn't learned.

She stumbled.

The audience gasped—a flock of air sucked in at once.

In the black gloss of the piano lid, her reflection lifted its chin to match her line. It blinked.

Not her.

A porcelain face peered back, cheeks too smooth, lips too red, eyes like buttons sunk deep in velvet night.

The reflection smiled wider than a mouth.

Escape or Entrapment

Emily broke the line and staggered offstage. The air behind the curtain was colder, wetter. The shadows followed, dragging like a train.

Dance forever... said a voice that wasn't a voice, velvet ever heard of.

The dark swelled up to swallow her. Something cold brushed her calf—like a glove full of water.

But then a hand seized her wrist. Human. Hot.

Mr. Greeley yanked her through the side door into the corridor, and the world snapped back into fluorescent hum.

"Not yet," he said, voice rough as gravel. Rain had freckled his shoulders though they were inside.

"You're lucky. This one wants a dancer… but she needs a host."

Emily swallowed. "She wanted—me?"

He raised his gloved hand.

"The dance," he said, and somewhere behind the door the piano played a note by itself, "has only just begun."

CHAPTER NINE

HYMN: The Doll That Sings in Shadows

"A lullaby soft, a whisper thin,
Beware the doll that sings Hymn.
Her song will soothe, then steal your breath,
Singing slow... a tune of death."

. . .

The Attic Discovery

The school was quiet at night. The halls kept their cold. Lockers clicked as they cooled, like teeth in a glass.

Mr. Greeley climbed the creaking stairs to the attic. He'd avoided this place for years.

Tonight felt different. Something tugged. Something he had tried to bury under work and dust.

In the corner, beneath a tarp the color of old bones, waited an oak chest.

Inside, wrapped in yellowed lace, lay a doll unlike any other.

Porcelain skin cracked delicately, webbed fractures that caught the light.

Eyes closed, as if listening. Tiny hands clutching a brass-key music box.

Mr. Greeley's swallow stuck in his throat. "Hymn," he whispered.

The Forgotten Song

He turned the key, careful as prayer.

A melody slid into the room, soft, sad, haunting.

Notes like breath on glass.

It raised a ghost: his daughter's laugh; her humming in the bath; the lullaby before sleep.

His chest ached.

Under the beauty, a cold thread pulled tight. The attic darkened at the edges.

Shadows drew long, as if the song gave them legs.

The Curse Revealed

Memory snapped him back: the storm, the fire, the doll in Lila's lap humming when no one touched it.

Smoke. Splintering glass. The last breath in a room that wouldn't cool.

The music stopped that night. The curse didn't.

Since then, children in town woke to the lullaby: soft voices in vents; a box on a sill no one placed there.

Those who listened too long slept differently; emptier.

Easier to move.

The First Victim

Emily, woke one midnight to a song so sweet it made her teeth ache. The music was sweet but faint.

On the windowsill sat a small box. She wound the key.

The room filled with sound. Her eyes fluttered closed.

In her dream, she danced through a forest of hanging ribbons. They weren't ribbons. They were shadows, reaching.

When she woke, she felt hollow behind the eyes, as if something had borrowed space and hadn't returned it.

She felt empty. Lost.

Mr. Greeley's Warning

Mr. Greeley had spent years hunting these dolls, locking them away.

Hymn was different. She didn't just haunt dreams, she harvested them.

He wrapped the doll in lace and lowered the lid. The lock clicked like a quiet throat.

As he turned the key: "Beware the lullaby. She doesn't soothe. She steals whatever listens too long."

The Shadow of the Past

That night, alone by the boiler-room stove, his hands shook in their gloves.

He studied the photo of Lila, paint on her knuckles, gap-toothed grin.

"I'm sorry," he whispered to a room that didn't answer.

Up in the attic, under the closed lid, something clicked.

Hymn's eyes fluttered open.

The lullaby began again, so soft the dust remembered the words.

CHAPTER TEN

WHISPER: The Doll That Speaks Secrets

"Whisper soft, a secret kept,
In silent rooms where shadows slept.
Listen close, but do beware,
Secrets told will lead to despair."

. . .

The thrift store on Maple Street breathed dust. The bell over the door had forgotten how to ring.

On a rain-lashed afternoon, a wooden crate appeared behind the counter. Mr. Langley didn't remember signing for it.

Inside, wrapped in brittle newsprint, lay a doll.

Faded cotton dress with tiny purple flowers. Lips sewn shut with thick black thread. Glass eyes dark and watchful.

A tiny silver locket at her throat, locked tight.

Mr. Langley set her on a back shelf, unaware the silence had learned his name.

Tara's Curiosity

Tara loved treasure hunts, the kind where you find a story and it chooses you.

She saw the doll in the window and felt the tug. Her mother bought it as a birthday gift.

That night, Tara placed the doll on her bedside table.

The room held its breath.

A sound brushed her ear, thin as floss.

"I know your secret..."

The First Whisper

Tara sat up. "Who's there?"

The doll's sewn lips seemed tighter. The voice arrived again, a little louder:

"I know what you hide."

Her mind sprinted to the worry she told no one, that move to a new school next year.

"How do you know?"

"You can't hide from me," whispered Whisper.

The Power Grows

Days later, the voice was bold enough to finish her thoughts.

Answers to tests Tara hadn't studied for, the name of the girl she liked, the real reason her best friend had gone cold, Whisper knew everything.

Each confession brightened those glass eyes.

It felt like being read, page after page, making her scared.

The Danger

Tara dreamed of a room with no doors. The shadows were shaped like people who wouldn't speak.

Whisper's voice skimmed the walls: "Tell no one... or lose what you hold most dear."

She woke sweating.

The doll's sewn mouth had curved.

The next day, she was missing things: her necklace; a family photo; the date of her best friend's birthday.

Not just objects. Pieces.

The Warning

Word traveled faster than secrets. Mr. Greeley knocked after dark.

"This one feeds on secrets and fear," he said, opening a leather notebook crowded with sketches. "The more you share, the stronger she gets."

"How do I stop her?"

"Starve the voice. And cage it when it screams."

Remember "You have to fight back. Don't let her take everything from you."

The Plan to Fight Back

Together they sketched a circle of salt on Tara's floor.

Mr. Greeley set down old charms and an iron cage no bigger than a breadbox.

Tara practiced silence, breathing through the whispers without answering.

It was like holding your breath under a heavy blanket.

Whisper's voice sweetened, promising to keep every secret safe, if Tara just told one more.

Tara didn't answer. She shrugged the softness of the doll.

She was strong.

The Final Confrontation

A storm hammered the roof one night. The doll's eyes flared red behind glass.

"Give me your secrets, Tara. Give me your fears."

Determined to finish the curse, Tara poured a line of salt. The air hissed as the grains hit carpet.

She lowered the iron cage over the doll.

Whisper screamed, a thin, needled sound that stitched itself through the room.

The cage thudded. The light dimmed. The voice frayed to a thread and snapped.

A New Beginning

Silence returned in layers.

Tara felt her memories file back into place.

Her necklace glinted under the bed. Her best friend texted. The window looked like a window again.

Mr. Greeley managed a tired smile. "You did well. Remember, these dolls rest like sharks. Eyes open."

Tara nodded, listening to the quiet.

CHAPTER ELEVEN

Velvet Vee: The Doll That Dances with Shadows – Part II

"Velvet whispers in the night,
Shadows dance just out of sight.
Spin the doll and hold your breath—
Dance with Vee or face your death."

. . .

The antique shop hid in the fold of a side street. Claire wandered in from the cold. The air smelled like mothballs and rosewater. Lamps wore yellow shades like bruises.

On a shelf crowded with saints and teacups sat a doll in deep crimson velvet. Pale porcelain skin. Black eyes that seemed to learn her face.

The shopkeeper, with silver hair and a voice that didn't bother the dust, placed the doll in Claire's hands.

“Velvet Vee,” she said. “Be careful. She dances for whom she chooses.”

Claire smiled because that is what you do in a store when your palms have already decided. She took the doll home.

The Dance Begins

That night, Claire set Velvet Vee on the dresser and turned off the lamp.

At midnight, a piano began to play somewhere near but not in the house. The song was slow and polite.

Claire woke up and saw shadows along the baseboards tugging at the corners like cats. They stood up. They stretched.

Claire’s feet slid across the floor. First one step, then another. Her body followed the rhythm that wasn’t playing on any device.

She tried to lock her knees. Her legs answered the music instead. She spun as if a hand were at her back.

Around her, the shadows spun too, a chorus of black partners that knew the steps better than she did.

In the mirror, she caught it. Velvet Vee's head had tilted. The doll's shadow was darker than the others, and it did not match the lamp.

Suddenly, the piano missed a note.
The shadows stopped.
The room let out a breath.

Claire blinked and found herself standing in the middle of the floor, toes cold on the boards. Her knees shook. She wrapped her arms around herself and tried to breathe slowly.

The lamp flickered once and stayed on. The walls were quiet again. No music. No movement. Only the tick of the clock.

She looked at the dresser.

Velvet Vee sat where Claire had left her. Head tilted. Eyes dark. Still.

Claire backed onto the bed and pulled the blanket to her chin. She told herself it had been a dream. She told herself she was safe.

In the silence, the air in the hallway carried one thin note, fading like a breath on glass.

The Curse Revealed

In the morning, Claire told Marcus everything. He believed the part about the music because he had heard it through the vent while brushing his teeth.

He did not believe the part about the shadows until she showed him the scuff marks on the floor where her slippers had dragged their own track in circles.

They started with the obvious search and worked backward. The doll turned up in a forum thread that felt like a dare, then in a scanned pamphlet at the library, tucked into a folder of local scandals.

The name Madame Borscht appeared twice. Once, as a costume maker for a turn-of-the-century ballet. Once in a note about a police raid at a warehouse full of unfinished dolls.

In the margin, someone had written in careful pencil: The shadow must be trapped in its reflection. Break the partner, and the dance will fail.

They copied the line while making a plan. They read it out loud until the words felt like a rule.

The Trap

At dusk, they bought four cheap mirrors and a spool of thin silver thread from the bead shop on Alder.

Marcus found an old program in a box of junk from the theater, a page torn and folded with a short prayer scrawled on the back. Claire braided the thread into three strands.

The apartment smelled like dust and lemon cleaner. They set the mirrors facing inward at the corners of the rug and poured a ring of salt, careful and slow, so there were no gaps.

“Stand in the middle,” Marcus said.

“I know,” Claire said. Her voice was steady. Her hands were not.

They waited without talking. The clock on the stove clicked from eleven fifty-nine to midnight. The first piano note arrived like a polite knock on the door.

Then another. The song unfolded, slow and sweet. Claire’s breath shortened. Her calves tightened. When the music asked for a step, her body obeyed.

She lifted her arms, and the shadows along the baseboard lifted theirs. It felt like someone else remembered the steps for her.

“Stay inside the salt,” Marcus said. His voice was small and careful, as if the air could hear it.

Velvet Vee watched from the dresser. The eyes were not bright. They were deep, like a hallway that did not end.

Claire turned with the melody. The mirrors multiplied the room until it looked like a hundred rooms, each with a Claire inside, each with a door that opened only toward her. The darkest shadow reached for her hand. Its fingers were thin and sure.

Claire let it draw close. She gave it one small step, then another, and guided it toward the nearest mirror. The glass held the reflection like a pond holds a face. The shadow bent to meet its own shape.

"Now," Claire whispered.

Marcus threw the silver net. The braid flashed once as it spread. It fell over Velvet Vee and tightened on its own, a fine, bright web. The room lurched as if a train had hit its brakes. The piano missed two notes and tried to find the tune again. It could not.

Everything stopped.

The shadows froze in half turns and then slid back into the floor and wall as if the house were tired of holding them. The mirrors showed only the room and the two of them, and the ring of salt.

Velvet Vee's eyes lost their depth, like shutters closing from inside.

Claire dropped to her knees. Her legs trembled. She laughed once, a breath that sounded like a cough. Marcus pressed his palm to the rug to make sure it was real. The clock ticked. The music stayed gone.

From the corner came a soft sound, fabric against fabric, like velvet turning over. A small laugh followed, not Claire's, not Marcus's. They both looked up at the same time.

The doll's hands sat where they had always been, folded and neat. But the shadow at her feet did not return to the floor

It had climbed, thin as smoke, and clung to the ceiling where the plaster cracked in hairlines. It was not alone. Three other shapes gathered there, faces rubbed smooth by distance, watching the bright circle of salt like hungry people watch a closed door.

Claire's mouth went dry. Marcus didn't speak. The piano did not start again, but the room remembered the song, and the memory moved across the ceiling like wind over tall grass.

CHAPTER TWELVE

Mr. Greeley's Last Stand

"Old man's secrets, lost and grim,

Faces haunted, future dim.

Janitor's fight with cursed delight,

Can he stop the endless night?"

. . .

The Janitor's Burden

Mr. Greeley kept Maple Elementary clean. That was what everyone saw. What no one saw was the room under the boiler where he hid wooden boxes lined with salt and iron.

He had learned the hard way that some toys do not rest when you throw them out.

Years ago, he had a family. A wife who sang while she cooked. A daughter named Lila, who drew faces in the fog on the car window.

Then the dolls came. They did not knock. They took. After the fire, he wore gloves to work and never slept all the way through night.

Haunted Memories

On a quiet evening, he sat in his small apartment. The walls held old photos that leaned a little in their frames. He traced Lila's smile with his thumb. He could still hear the tune from the music box she loved.

He could still smell the smoke. He whispered, "I am sorry," to the empty room, and the empty room kept it.

The Breaking Point

That week, the school felt wrong. Water alarms went off with no leaks. Doors swelled at the bottom as if they had been rained on from the inside.

In the sandbox behind the swings, small prints appeared and disappeared. He swept them. They came back. Doll-sized. Pointing toward the gate.

Mr. Greeley was certain something or someone was pulling the strings.

Night came, and he took inventory the way he always did before a hunt. A silver knife polished with salt. A jar of holy water. Three small charms he had cut from church pew wood and scratched with tiny prayers. A coil of iron wire. A wooden box with filings glued to the inside like glitter from a bad craft project.

He knew it was not enough. He went anyway, straight to the playground.

Wind pulled at the swings. The field was a dark sheet. He stepped into the sandbox and felt the sand shift under his boots like something breathing.

A rag doll sat in the middle, one button eye, the other a torn nest of threads.

"Miss Mumu," he said, as if the sand needed the name.

The doll's mouth did not move. The sand around her did. It mounded and slumped, slow as tides.

He quickly drew a circle on the sand with the knife. He stepped inside and recited the ancient incantations. The wind dropped. Sounds backed away.

A shape lifted behind the doll. It rose like steam and then took weight. It reached the height of a child and then became taller.

It tried to make a face. It tried to make Lila's face. He did not look. He did not give it that.

He set the jar at his feet and the three charms at the edges of the circle. He looped the iron wire three times and said his daughter's name once, the way you say a word you do not lend to anyone.

The shadow hit the circle and broke like a wave on glass.

Light and dark ran against each other. It felt like he was keeping a door shut with his whole back while a flood pushed from the other side.

Sand sprayed up and stung his cheeks. The knife hummed in his hand as if it wanted to leave.

The shadow leaned in. It could not touch him while he spoke, so it tried to take his words. Mr. Greeley was overwhelmed, and there he made a desperate choice.

He used a binding spell. trapping the spirits inside a sealed box- sacrificing a part of his own soul to keep the curse contained.

He threw the wire. It tightened as if it knew how. The shadow thinned and folded, slow, the way fire folds paper when it is almost finished. He pushed the doll and the shadow into the wooden box.

He closed the lid. The lock clicked like a last step on a stair.

He sat down hard in the sand. The night returned in pieces. The swings moved again.

The fence rattled once and forgot. He felt older. He felt empty. Dawn found him like that and made him stand.

A Warning to All

In the morning, he told the office that there had been a plumbing issue and the playground was closed for repairs. He taped a sign on the door to the basement that said KEEP OUT. He meant it every way a person can mean it.

He carried the box to the room under the boiler and set it on a shelf with others that did not shake when buses passed.

He wrote a label in small block letters: MUMU — BINDED AT SANDBOX. COST: SECRET. He put the pen down and waited to feel like himself. It did not happen.

That afternoon, he stood in front of the school. The kids flowed past him in noisy lines. He watched the faces, counting without thinking.

He did not see Lila's face, and he did not expect to, but he looked anyway. He cleared his throat and raised his voice so it would carry.

"Listen up," he said. "If anyone brings a doll to school, it goes to the office. If anyone finds a doll on the grounds, do not touch it. Call me first. If you hear singing where there is no song, you come find a grown-up. If water shows up where it should not, you tell someone with keys."

Teachers nodded. Kids giggled because that is what kids do when fear and rules meet in the same hallway. Mr. Greeley let them. He did not smile.

He took one last look at the sky. A band of cloud stretched thin as old gauze. He could feel the weight of every box below his feet.

He knew the work was not done. It would not be done while he was alive. He pulled on his gloves and went back inside to make another circle of salt that no one would see and everyone would need.

CHAPTER THIRTEEN

The Secret of Madame Borscht

"In shadows deep, a secret lies,
A witch's curse beneath the skies.
Dolls that move and spirits trapped,
The curse begins where time has snapped."

. . .

One night, the rain drummed against the grimy windows of Mr. Greeley's small apartment above Maple Street Elementary. Dust drifted in the lamplight, settling on stacks of old books and faded photographs.

Claire and Tara sat across from him on the sagging couch. Curiosity held them in place. Fear kept them still.

Mr. Greeley opened a heavy leather book that looked older than the building. The gold letters still showed through the cracks: The Legend of Madame Borscht.

His voice stayed low. "Madame Borscht was a witch, centuries ago," he said. " She lived in a village far from here, deep inside a dense forest no one dared enter."

Claire's shoulders tightened about the eerie tale.

"The villagers were afraid of her work," he went on. "They were right to be. Her dolls weren't toys. They were vessels." He turned a page with care.

"She trapped souls. The lost. The angry. She thought she could make them serve her."

His finger rested on a drawing of a long table crowded with half-made dolls, mouths unfinished, eyes waiting. "Instead, she taught them to wander, forever trapped and angry."

The Witch's Downfall

"One day, the people burned the workshop," Mr. Greeley said. "They watched the roof fall in and the chimney break. They thought the fire would clean the wood."

"It didn't."

Flames ate the house but left the work. The dolls rolled out under the smoke and scattered like rats. They hitched rides in carts and trunks. Some people bought them. Some found them at the bottom of boxes where nothing should be.

“They learned,” he said, “To feed on fear. On pain. On secrets. Each one carries a piece of her craft.”

He unfolded a thin map tucked in the binding, an old, fragile paper soft as old cloth. Strange symbols marked a path through a forest just outside town, a path that seemed to move even on the page.

“This is where she began. If an end exists,” he said, “it will be there.”

Tara swallowed. “They won’t let us near it. This is too dangerous.”

“Yes,” he said. “They’ll try their best to pull us apart before we find the door.”

Claire said. “But if we don’t stop it... more kids could get hurt. This is a far greater risk than not doing anything.”

Mr. Greeley exhaled, “Yes. We have no other choice.”

Gathering the Tools

They started gathering the materials for the next two days and didn't talk about it. Mr. Greeley sharpened a silver knife and rubbed it with salt.

He filled small glass bottles with holy water blessed under the full moon. He carved charms from old stone.

Tara poured salt into plastic tubs and labeled each with a black marker.

PROTECT. BIND. LAST CHANCE.

The trio kept preparing, finding jars and bottles that would come in handy.

On the third day, after sunset, they set out. The trees at the edge of the forest leaned together like people telling a secret. The air went quieter as they moved forward.

No bird talk. No insect hum. Their steps sounded wrong, as if the ground had been carpeted for someone else.

The map led and then didn't. Trails bent back on themselves. A branch brushed Claire's cheek with the care of a hand she did not want.

From time to time, something laughed, soft and far away, and then closer.

Tara muttered the short prayer she'd copied onto her palm while wiping her sweat. Mr. Greeley touched each tree trunk with his glove as if counting them into witness.

Suddenly, a soft, eerie laughter drifted through the air, as if it had been following them for long.

The Plague Doctor Doll

From behind a twisted oak stepped a small figure. Shadow Pox, the plague doctor doll.

His rusted beak mask hid his face. Glass eyes watched them without blinking.

A cold mist poured from his sleeves and spread across the ground. It wrapped Tara's legs. Her breath shortened, and her eyes went white

Tara cried out and stumbled. Claire grabbed her arm and pulled her back.

Mr. Greeley moved first. He drew a silver knife and cut through the fog in short, clean strokes. The mist pulled away from the blade as if it knew the metal.

"Salt," he said.

Tara scattered salt in wide arcs, steadying her hand.

Claire uncorked a bottle of holy water and swept it in a tight circle. Drops flashed and hung in the mist like bright pins.

Mr. Greeley began a short prayer. He kept his voice low and even. The words shook the branches above them.

The doll shrieked, a thin, sharp sound. Its shape broke apart into strips of shadow and blew back into the trees.

They stood still and waited for the quiet to return. When it did, they caught their breath and moved on.

The Workshop

The forest opened without warning.

A low stone cabin crouched in a hollow. Its walls were blackened by age and old magic. Twisted vines covered the windows like hands that would not let go. From inside, a faint glow pulsed.

They stepped through the doorway.

Shelves lined the room. Heads, hands, and unfinished bodies waited for someone who would not return. Threads hung from the rafters like webbing that had learned to braid itself.

In the center sat the largest doll of all. The Mother Doll.

Her face was cracked in fine lines. Her eyes burned with an old red light.

A voice filled the room. It sounded close and far at the same time. "You cannot end the curse. You only feed it."

Shadows rose behind her like curtains, finding their shape. The room narrowed to the three of them and her.

The nightmares began at once. Tara saw a classroom where every face had empty eyes. Claire felt hands catch her ankles. Mr. Greeley heard a lullaby come up a stair and stop at a door that would not open.

But none of this stopped them.

Mr. Greeley held the leather book in one hand and the knife in the other. He spoke prayers that made his throat ache. Claire and Tara dodged the shadows and threw salt and holy water to break their reach.

The Mother Doll laughed without smiling. The glow in her chest brightened.

Behind a broken loom, at the back wall, a crystal pulsed. It was dark and smoky, and it fed a thin thread of light into the Mother Doll.

"There," Claire said.

Mr. Greeley saw it too. He lowered his shoulder and moved through the room while the nightmares tried to press him flat.

He reached the heart of the workshop. An ancient crystal. It glowed with dark magic.

Shattering the Crystal

He lifted his knife and brought it down with both hands. The crystal cracked. Then it shattered.

The workshop shook. Shelves rattled. Dolls screamed, a mix of anger and sorrow, unexplainable voices.

Light spilled from the broken stone and ran across the floor like quicksilver. The Mother Doll's eyes dimmed. Her lids lowered as if heavy with sleep.

One by one, the other dolls turned to flickers of light and rose, tiny sparks drifting toward the roof and out into the pale sky.

The forest let out a breath; it felt light.

They walked out at first light. The trees looked like trees again.

Mr. Greeley let a small smile show. “The dolls are gone,” he said. “But their stories remain.”

Claire looked at Tara and then at Mr. Greeley. None of them would forget what they had seen.

CHAPTER FOURTEEN

Echoes in the Dark

"Beneath the floor, a whisper calls,
Shadows crawl along the walls.
Secrets lost and voices tossed,
What's the price? What's the cost?"

. . .

Returning Home

The sun had barely set when Claire and Tara reached Tara's porch. Their nerves still rang from what they had done in the workshop. The dolls should be gone. They hoped so.

The house was quiet in a way that did not feel like peace. The clock in the kitchen ticked, but the sound seemed swallowed. The air felt heavy, cool against their arms.

Tara set her backpack down and listened. Pipes clicked once in the walls. Floorboards sighed. In the far hallway, a thin voice threaded the quiet.

"Help me..."

They turned the corner together in fear, with sweat on their face.

A doll sat at the base of the stairs.

Not one they knew. Small face with a smile looking at them. The dress was old, high collar, the fabric covered with dust as if it had not moved in years.

Claire crouched. “Where did this come from?”

Tara shook her head. “I locked the door. No one’s been here.”

They checked the latch. The deadbolt had been thrown from the inside.

A Voice in the Dark

The doll’s head turned, a small, neat motion. The eyes blinked as if they had found them and held tight.

The lips did not part, but a voice filled the hall, soft and close, as if it came from under the floor.

“I’m lost... but I remember.”

Claire flinched and looked for a speaker. There was none.

“Who are you?” Tara asked, barely above a whisper.

"Lila, the lost doll from Mr. Greeley's past," the voice said.

"How did you get here?" Tara said.

"I followed you after escaping the ruins of the workshop. I came through cracks. I hid in your vents, in the crawl space, and in the quiet corners of this house," said Lila.

"The curse isn't over," Lila added. "The big doll fell, but not all the small ones were inside when it happened. Some learned to live between walls, others fled, and they are coming."

A soft bump sounded under the living-room floor, then another, as if someone was approaching from very far.

Tara steadied herself on the banister. "Are they coming here?"

"They wander," Lila said. "They like secrets. They like empty places inside people. They saw the light on."

Claire swallowed. "We need Mr. Greeley."

"You will," Lila said while her voice got thinner as she disappeared gradually into the dark.

The heat left the hallway. Claire looked at Tara. Tara looked at the front door and then back, looking for the doll that seemed to have gone into hiding.

Sighing, they chose the same next step without speaking: find Mr. Greeley, make a plan, don't let the house choose for them.

They gathered their things while constantly feeling supervised, as if someone was waiting for them.

CHAPTER FIFTEEN

The Hunt Begins

"Dolls hide where darkness clings,
In broken toys and rusted strings.
Hunt them down, don't look away,
Or join the night and fade away."

. . .

Mr. Greeley's Revelation

Mr. Greeley sat by the heater while the coil glowed. The light crawled along the walls like shadows deciding where to rest.

He pulled a leather bag into his lap and opened it. Notes, photos, and small relics slid into view. A folded map, patched and taped, lay on top.

"This," he said, "is where we look next."

Claire and Tara leaned in as he smoothed the map across the table. Names were inked at the edges with short marks beside them:

- Whisper — the stalker of silence.

- Hymn — the lullaby that traps dreams.
- Shadow Pox — the plague doctor that spreads fear like sickness.

"We've tracked sightings," he said. "They hide in abandoned places- playgrounds, old houses, forgotten corners"

They packed the same tools because the rules had not changed: silver blades, salt, holy water, and a coil of iron wire. Tara's hands shook when she tied the bag. Her eyes stayed steady.

She hadn't recovered from the last encounter, but time wasn't on her side.

"First stop," Greeley said, tapping a square on the map. "The old school at the edge of town. Whisper has been seen there."

The building was locked, but not guarded. Windows boarded. Paint peeled in long strips like old tape. Their steps echoed down halls lined with broken desks and empty boards.

Cold air pooled in the corners. Sounds brushed past their ears, without a word.

Claire felt eyes watching from every shadow.

In the music room, the piano sat with its lid open. A shape slid across the floor without sound and came to rest in front of them.

Whisper. Totally calm. Lips sewn shut. Eyes caught the thin hall light.

She glided, then stopped. The voice arrived without a mouth to carry it, a whisper that bent their thoughts toward worry they had tried to put away.

Greeley poured a strip of salt across the warped wood, creating a protective barrier.

Whisper recoiled as if the grain burned. The hiss came thin and fast.

"Net," Greeley said.

Claire lifted the silver mesh he had made and flicked it wide. Tara kept the line of salt unbroken while the doll searched for a gap.

The net fell. It tightened on its own, bright and fine. Whisper's eyes flashed once. She shrieked without opening her mouth and turned to mist that folded in on itself and was gone.

They waited for the quiet to return. It did, layer by layer.

Mr. Greeley set the bag on his shoulder. “Two remain,” he said. “And they won’t come this easily.”

Claire closed her hand over the knife. “We keep going.”

CHAPTER SIXTEEN

Hymn's Lullaby

"A broken tune drifts through the night,

Soft and sweet but filled with fright.

Close your eyes, don't make a peep,

Or fall into the endless sleep."

. . .

Heading to the Old Music Hall

The trio's next stop was the abandoned music hall at the edge of town. People said Hymn lived there now, the doll with the lullaby that wouldn't end.

The once-grand theater was overgrown with ivy and swallowed by darkness. As they stepped inside, the silence went past quiet into heavy. No creak. No wind. Only stillness that pressed on their chests.

Then a sound rose from the stage, a thin melody, slow and off-key, like an old music box trying to remember a tune. It kept increasing as they got closer to the stage.

Moonlight touched the boards, and Hymn sat in its pool. A cracked bonnet shaded a porcelain face. She rocked, small and steady, thumb and finger winding a brass-key box that clicked before each phrase.

The lullaby drifted through the empty seats and echoed off the walls. It wrapped Claire and Tara in something soft and cold. Claire's eyelids sagged. Her knees loosened. The floor seemed to lift and offer to hold her.

"Stay awake," Tara whispered, shaking her once, twice, but the music leaned harder. Mr. Greeley's voice cut through it: "Hymn steals dreams first."

Tara yanked a silver bell from the kit and rang it hard. The note bit the air and cracked the song.

The melody broke. Hymn's eyes flared in rage. The doll tipped from the stage and moved towards them.

They ran the aisles to escape from the Hymn wrath. Seats snagged their coats. A ceiling beam groaned and dropped dust like ash.

Claire stumbled on a split board and went down. Hymn came closer, repeating a lullaby.

"Water," Greeley snapped. Tara swept holy water in a bright arc while he cast silver dust that hung in the air like filings and clung to the doll's dress.

Hymn screeched. The song wavered, and her loud voice echoed throughout the hall.

Claire's hand struck something under a ripped velvet seat while hiding from the doll: a broken music box. She grabbed it and smashed it against Hymn's as she moved near her.

The lullaby stopped mid-note.

Hymn stiffened. A breathless second held. Then the doll folded inward and fell to pale shards.

The theater remembered how to be quiet.

They stood until the dust settled. Claire wiped grit from her palms. Tara lowered the bell. Mr. Greeley scanned the catwalks before he spoke. "One more gone," he said. "But listen."

A whisper slid through the rafters, thin as thread: "You can stop me, but others will play..."

They did not answer it. They checked their salt at the door, stepped over it, and left the hall to its silence.

CHAPTER SEVENTEEN

Shadow Pox's Cold Grip

"From darkest mist and frozen breath,
Comes chilling touch and silent death.
Beware the plague that spreads in the night,
Or vanish in the fading light."

. . .

Into the Frozen Swamp

People said the last doll hid near the old swamp. No one went there after sundown. The fog was thick along the banks, and the cold felt wrong in a way that had nothing to do with the weather.

Frost sheeted the bent trees when the trio arrived. Heavy mist curled over the black water and climbed the roots, and the world looked smeared like a picture rubbed with a thumb.

Claire pulled her jacket tight and tried to steady her breath. Tara kept close, her own breath lifting in white bursts. Mr. Greeley scanned the reeds as if the swamp would answer if he watched long enough.

A shape gathered in the fog and pulled it tight as it stepped forward. The rusted beak caught the little light. Glass eyes held steady. Shadow Pox.

Icy vapor poured from the pointed mask and slid over the ground until it touched their boots.

The air seized. Tara's fingers went numb, and a stitch of pain tightened in her chest. Claire felt a slow frost push under her ribs and spread.

Shadow Pox breathed again. Frost skinned the ground, and thin cracks raced across a shallow pool, knitting a hard sheet between the hummocks. Claire slipped and caught herself on a root slick with ice.

"Keep cover and keep moving," Mr. Greeley said.

He spoke a short spell, and heat pulsed in the air, opening a narrow path through the ice. Tara threw salt in wide arcs that hissed where the grains struck.

The doll glided, faded, then reformed farther off. It was quick, and it kept the cold on them, a steady weight that made each step clumsy and each breath heavy.

The swamp pushed back. Trees leaned toward the path. Water rose against the roots and nudged them off course. Ways forward closed and then opened again, as if the place had a mind and did not want them there.

"There," Claire said. The fog thinned over a flat span of ice that looked sound. It rang a little underfoot, hollow and hard.

They spread out and crossed slowly, testing each step. Shadow Pox followed without sound.

Mr. Greeley took out a silver net and handed one edge to Tara. Claire drew out a small charm etched with a fire mark and felt it warm in her palm.

"Draw her in," Mr. Greeley said. He backed away and let his voice carry. The doll followed the thread of sound.

They raised the net. The mesh dropped over the doll and tightened when they pulled it together.

Frost cracked under the weight. The glass eyes flashed once and dulled. The cold pressed harder, one last push that shook their knees.

Mr. Greeley spoke the final spell. Claire touched the hot charm to the mesh. Fire ran through the lines like quick light.

The ice boomed and lifted steam. The net glowed and then went dark. Shadow Pox shattered. Pieces hissed and slid into the pond like salt in rain.

Mist loosened its hold on the trees. The swamp let out a long sigh, the sound of a place tired of holding its breath.

They stood until the shaking left their legs. Dawn took the sky a little at a time.

"It is done," Mr. Greeley said. He did not smile.

They turned to go. In the mud by the bank, a thin shard of porcelain showed under the water. It caught a thread of light and then went dull again.

CHAPTER EIGHTEEN

The Mother Doll's Return

"The mother waits with eyes aflame,
Her whispers call the cursed name.
Break her seal or face the night,
Forever trapped in endless fright."

. . .

The Calm Before the Storm

With Shadow Pox gone and the others captured or broken, it should have been over. Claire and Tara wanted to believe it. Mr. Greeley did not.

"There is one more," he said. "The Mother Doll."

They went back to the ruined workshop in the woods. The stones were black, and the windows were covered by vines. The air held old smoke and something older.

Inside, the room felt larger than before, as if the walls had stepped back to make space for what waited there.

The Mother Doll sat at the center of a cracked wooden chair. Lines split her porcelain face like dry riverbeds, and a slow red glow moved behind the breaks.

A dark crystal hung at her chest. It pulsed. The room seemed to lean toward it and draw its weight from its light.

"We end it by ending that," Mr. Greeley said. He meant the crystal.

The doll's eyes opened, and she stood. Her joints moved smoothly. The voice that filled the room was soft and cold.

"You cannot destroy me. I am the mother of fear."

The Battle Begins

Claire and Tara kept moving. The doll's fingers were sharp as broken dishes. Mr. Greeley spoke a steady spell while moving towards the doll.

Shadows gathered in the rafters and dropped around them on long ropes. The crystal on the doll's chest took every strike meant for her.

Each blow came back as a dark wave that made their bones buzz, and their teeth ached.

The pattern showed itself. When the doll fixed on one of them, the crystal brightened. When her focus split, the light dimmed, and the push weakened.

"We need distraction," Tara said. She stepped left and clapped once to catch the eye. Claire moved right and laid a clean line of salt. Mr. Greeley widened the ring along with her until the circle felt shut.

The doll turned faster. Anger climbed. She went after Tara into the open space. Claire and Mr. Greeley finished the ring and closed it tight.

"Hold your places," Mr. Greeley said. He lifted the book and the silver knife while saying the spell as fast as he could.

The Mother Doll struck the edge of the circle while chasing Tara back inside. The salt flared. The crystal flickered.

"Now," he said.

Claire went in low and quick and drove the silver point at the crystal.

The stone cracked. Light poured out in a hot rush. She struck again.

The crystal shattered, and white light filled the room. The floor shook and the shelves rattled. Many voices rose and then fell away to nothing.

Mother Doll's eyes dimmed. Porcelain split and fell into quiet pieces. The red glow went out, and the room let go of its breath.

Shadows thinned like smoke in a clean wind. The pressure broke, and the workshop felt small again.

They waited in the doorway and let the air clear. Outside, the trees looked like trees. The path looked like a path.

"The curse is broken," Mr. Greeley said. His voice was tired and sure.

They walked into the morning. For the first time in years, the forest felt clean.

CHAPTER NINETEEN

Home At Last

"Safe inside, the night grows deep,

But secrets in the dark still creep.

Locks and bolts cannot keep them out,

When dolls still whisper and shadows shout."

. . .

Returning to Normal

Days later, the town looked the same, and life tried to follow. Claire and Tara went back to their routine.

They laughed at lunch, walked home together, and talked about ordinary things as if the past weeks could be folded and put away.

Still, the house kept a quiet that did not feel like peace. When Claire passed the shelf of dolls, she felt a tug low in her chest, a reminder that stillness can hide a voice.

She told herself she was fine, and then found her eyes on the doll faces again.

One evening, the doorbell rang. Tara's mom found a small package on the mat with no name and no return. The paper was clean.

The twine was tight. Inside lay a tiny doll they had never seen. Her bonnet was tattered, and her glass eyes seemed to hold the light a second too long before letting it go.

Claire felt her heartbeat climb. The doll did not move, yet the room seemed to lean toward the box the way a room leans toward a storm.

Tara set the package on the table and stepped back as if the wood might give under her hands.

That night, a thin lullaby drifted along the hall. The tune was soft and sweet, but something in it pressed at the ribs.

It slipped under doors and turned the corners like a draft you cannot find. Claire sat up in bed and listened with both hands on the blanket, counting the notes to make sure they were real.

Near midnight, the phone rang. Mr. Greeley's voice came low and rough, and he did not waste words. "There are more," he said. "The curse learned how to sleep while it watches. Be careful."

The line clicked, and the house felt larger for a moment, as if the walls had stepped back to listen.

Shadows shifted where the stair rail met the wall. They stretched long and pulled short, like footsteps that did not want to be seen.

The doll's eyes caught a thread of moonlight from the window and gave it back a little brighter than before.

A whisper rose from the box. It was soft as breath against glass. "We are not done yet."

Claire stayed awake. Morning would come whether the night allowed it or not.

At first light, Claire hurried to Tara and told her everything. Tara listened, fingers laced with Claire's, and the same thought passed between them.

The road might bend again. The quiet might speak. If the dolls returned, they would face them together. And when the time came, they would be ready to answer.

CHAPTER TWENTY

The Quiet Dollhouse

"A dollhouse stands so neat, so still,
With tiny beds and windowsills.
But late at night, when no one's near,
The rooms fill up with screams and fear."

. . .

A Strange Invitation

Two days after the Mother Doll fell, a letter found Claire. The envelope was thick and creamy, her name written in a careful hand that looked older than the paper itself.

Inside, the message was brief.

> "Your work has reached my attention. Come at once. There are things you must see."

A train ticket slid from the fold, followed by a sealed note stamped in red wax. She told Tara, who begged her not to go and listed every reason to stay, but the note in Claire's palm felt like a door that had already opened.

Mr. Greeley did not try to stop her. He placed an old silver locket in her hand, closed her fingers around it, and said only, “Keep this with you.”

The same night, Tara boarded the train and reached a strange, deserted house. The dead trees made a crooked line against the sky. Wind moved through them without a rise or fall, more like a whisper than weather.

Inside, there were dolls. Hundreds. They sat in glass cases, on velvet risers, and along the tops of cabinets, arranged in perfect scenes, every face tipped toward the room as if waiting for a cue that had not yet been given.

Claire felt the skin lift along her arms and knew she had not come to the end of anything. She had come to the beginning of something older.

Madame Cressida

A woman appeared in the doorway without a sound. She was tall and spare, her white hair braided like a crown. Her voice stayed low, yet it carried.

“Madame Cressida, is that you?” asked Claire while wiping her sweat from her forehead.

“Yes. You survived the children’s dolls,” she said. “It is time to learn the history of the Ancients.”

Without breaking that calm tone, she turned, and Claire followed. They moved down a narrow side corridor where the glass cases gave way to wood doors and dark oil portraits that watched with flat eyes. Cressida opened one door and led her into a private room.

A dollhouse filled the space like a small building. It reached Claire's shoulder and stretched wall to wall.

At first, it seemed still. Then the stillness breathed. Lights flickered behind tiny windows. Little doors opened and closed on their own.

"They are alive," Claire said before she could stop herself.

"Each one holds a soul," Cressida answered. "Not all are cruel. Many are angry."

On the table beside the dollhouse lay a book wrapped in faded leather. Cressida lifted it with two hands and placed it in Claire's arms.

Flaking gold letters pressed into the cover read The Grimoire of Thread and Ash. The pages told of the Stitcher, the first maker, who gave up her own spirit to call motion into cloth and porcelain.

"She sewed grief into fiber," Cressida whispered, leaning close as if fear might overhear. "And the dolls have kept feeding."

Claire smoothed a page with her fingertips. The paper throbbed once like a pulse and gave a small dry scream. She pulled back, and the sound died, as if it had only been waiting for someone to touch it.

From inside the great dollhouse came a sharp crack. One tiny room split at the corner. A porcelain figure stirred and lifted its head.

Claire looked for the name in the compendium beside the book and did not find it. A black veil covered the face. When the fabric shifted, burned skin showed beneath, healed in a way that did not look like healing at all.

"Her name is Miss Maw," Cressida said. "She has not spoken since the fire."

The mansion lights failed as if the house had decided to hold its breath. In the dark that followed, the dolls turned their heads together, a single soft click of porcelain in many cases.

Claire ran. She held the Grimoire against her chest and followed the thin line of light that slipped under the door back into the hall. When she looked over her shoulder, Cressida was still in the room, ringed by glass and waking faces.

"Warn them," Cressida said from the dark. "They are not done."

CHAPTER TWENTY EXTENDED

Miss Maw Awakens

"When mouths are seen, the screams stay in.
When eyes are burned, the curse begins.
She waits in ash, she walks through flame,
And now she whispers your name."

. . .

Meanwhile, Across the Country

In a different town, seven year old Melody June found an old trunk in her grandmother's attic. Dust rose when she lifted the lid.

Inside lay a soot-stained doll with sewn lips and button eyes. A ribbon was tied tight around the doll's throat. A small tag hung from the knot, its writing faded but still clear enough to read one name.

Miss Maw.

Melody knew she should ask before touching it, but curiosity felt louder than the attic's silence. She untied the ribbon.

The attic drew a long breath and let it go in a single gasp. The lightbulb shattered with a dry pop. Shadows clung to the rafters as if the darkness had turned wet. The stitches at the doll's mouth cracked like thin ice.

"I remember the fire," a whisper said, and the sound drifted into the old wood as if the house had been waiting to hear it.

At the same hour, miles away, Tara came awake to a wrongness that did not belong to dreams.

Every stuffed animal on her bed had been turned to face the wall.

Every one.

Their backs made a soft line along the blanket like a row of small shoulders. The closet door creaked and eased open. The space inside smelled like dust and cold cloth.

"She has found a new one," a voice breathed from the dark, and Tara could not tell if it came from the closet or from inside her chest.

Across town, Claire was not sleeping either. She set the Grimoire on her desk and opened it to the last page they had checked before.

The paper was clean for a moment, then changed. Ink bled up from the fibers and began to write by itself. New names formed in a hand that shook and dragged. Each stroke looked like a cut that rose with blood.

The final page held still, waiting. Then a point of ink pricked the corner and pulled a line across the middle. Letters gathered, slow and certain, until a name stood where there had been nothing.

Miss Maw.

Back in the attic, Melody realized she was humming a lullaby she did not know. Her hands were empty. The doll was no longer on her lap. When she turned, she saw the shape by the window.

Miss Maw stood in the slice of moonlight with the veil gone and the face bare. The porcelain was burned in a way that made the smooth parts look like they were pretending not to hurt.

The eyes were open. The mouth was no longer sewn. The doll smiled as if she had practiced for years and had finally remembered how.

Somewhere else, by the light of one candle, a figure worked over a table. The room did not show its walls, only the circle of flame and the hands inside it.

A needle moved in a steady rhythm, up and down, pulling thread through a curve of fabric. Eyes were being sewn onto something too large to be a child's toy. Behind the worker, shelves held rows of blank bodies waiting for their turn.

"They burned the Mother," the figure. "They crushed the children. They forgot the Bride."

The worker turned toward the flame. Her mouth was stitched shut. Her eyes were bright. She smiled without parting the thread.

The dolls were not dead. They had been waiting. Now they were making more. And the first had already remembered her name.

"To Be Continued"

Made in the USA
Coppell, TX
18 February 2026